INCH and MILES

The Journey to Success

Coach John Wooden

with Steve Jamison
and Peanut Louie Harper

Illustrated by Susan F. Cornelison

more interested in finding the best way, not in having your way ✳ Control yourself so others won't have to ✳ What you learn after you
nd steady gets you ready ✳ Act, eat, and think right ✳ Practice makes perfect ✳ Be eager to help your team ✳ Just be yourself ✳ You m

Inch and Miles: The Journey to Success

Printed in Mexico. For information, contact
Perfection Learning® Corporation, 1000 North Second Avenue,
P.O. Box 500, Logan, Iowa 51546-0500.
Phone: 1-800-831-4190 • Fax: 1-800-543-2745
perfectionlearning.com

Editorial Director: Susan C. Thies
Design Director: Randy Messer
Illustrator: Susan F. Cornelison
Book Design: Tobi S. Cunningham
Color Specialist: Jane Wonderlin

(Back cover photo of Coach Wooden courtesy of Ev Edstrom.)

Library of Congress Cataloging-in-Publication Data

Wooden, John R.
Inch and Miles : the journey to success / by John Wooden
with Steve Jamison and Peanut Louie Harper.– 1st ed.
p. cm.
Summary: Inch and Miles toot a magic silver whistle to help them find clues to the pyramid of success.
ISBN 0-7569-1410-8 (hardcover) – ISBN 0-7891-6073-0 (pbk.)
[1. Success-Fiction. 2. Self-actualization-Fiction.]
I. Jamison, Steve.
II. Harper, Peanut Louie. III. Title.
PZ7.W8602 In 2003
[Fic]–dc21
2003005498

Also available from Coach John Wooden,

WOODEN: A Lifetime of Observations and Reflections

(McGraw-Hill)

4 5 6 RRD 07 06 05 04

ing to prepare is preparing to fail ✳ Make each day special ✳ To make friends, be a friend ✳ Be trustworthy ✳ Be more interested in fin
hurry ✳ Slow and steady gets you ready ✳ Act, eat, and think right ✳ Practice makes perfect ✳ Be eager to help your team ✳ Just be yo

is what counts ✳ Be quick, but don't hurry ✳ Slow and steady gets you ready ✳ Act, eat, and think right ✳ Practice makes perfect ✳ Be

in yourself if you expect others to believe in you ✳ Failing to prepare is preparing to fail ✳ Make each day special ✳ To make friends, be

Coach Wooden, Steve, and Peanut dedicate INCH and
MILES to the most important word in our dictionary: LOVE.

Special thanks to Nan Wooden Muehlhausen;
Tim, Casey, and Jared Harper; Ronald and Alice Louie;
Ev and Mary Jean Edstrom; Mike Cronen;
and Margo Sorenson.

A big thank-you to Cathleen Trapani for helping to make
INCH and MILES come true!

And, of course, this book is for Nellie Wooden.

st way, not in having your way ✳ Control yourself so others won't have to ✳ What you learn after you know it all is what counts ✳ Be q

ou must believe in yourself if you expect others to believe in you ✳ Failing to prepare is preparing to fail ✳ Make each day special ✳ To

It is the last day before summer vacation, and Inch and Miles have one final assignment. Their teacher, Mr. Wooden, has just written this question on the board:

What Is Success?

Miles tries first, "That's easy. Success is winning a shiny gold medal or trophy for first place!"

Mr. Wooden shakes his head.

Inch is quiet, but not for long. "Success is being the most popular kid at school and having the most friends."

A frown crosses Mr. Wooden's face.

So Inch and Miles try again, together. "Toys, Mr. Wooden. Success is having the best toys!"

"Inch and Miles," their teacher finally replies:

Success isn't having trophies or toys.
It isn't a medal or friends of your choice.
What is Success? That's easy to see.
It's trying to be the best *you* can be!
Don't worry what others may have or might say.
When trying your best,
Success comes your way.

Inch and Miles listen as Mr. Wooden continues. "Success is happiness in your heart because you try 100 percent to be your personal best. And no one can do that better than you."

Inch and Miles exchange puzzled looks. "But, Mr. Wooden, how do we try 100 percent to be our best?" Inch asks.

Mr. Wooden doesn't answer. Instead, he turns and slowly unlocks the drawer of his old oak desk. Carefully he removes a small bundle wrapped in a tattered green cloth. As Mr. Wooden unfolds the cloth, Inch and Miles see a sparkling silver whistle.

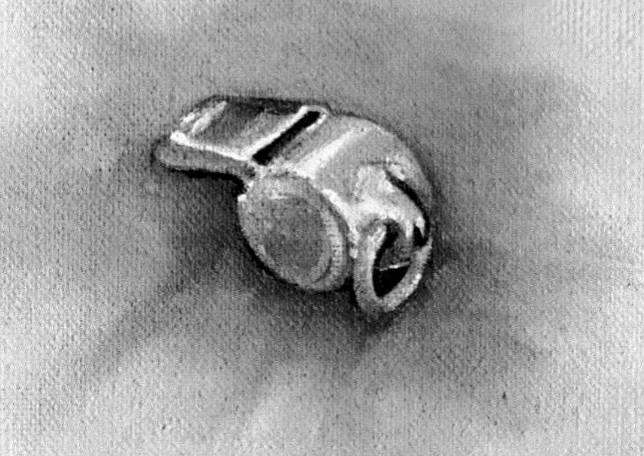

"This whistle is very special," Mr. Wooden tells Inch and Miles. "It can help you find the answer to your question. Take it to the edge of the school yard. You'll be surprised what happens when you give it a loud **HOOTIE-TOOT-TOOT!"**

Now Inch and Miles are really puzzled. How can a silver whistle teach them how to try 100 percent to be their best?

Mr. Wooden continues.

You'll meet special friends who are good teachers too.
Each one has a message especially for you.
To learn how to try 100 percent,
Just ask them for clues—you'll be glad that you went.
Then you will find my Pyramid of Success.
Each of its blocks helps bring out your best.
Listen and learn and do as they tell.
You'll then see Success as clear as a bell.

Inch and Miles can't wait to get started! A Pyramid of Success. How exciting! Soon they'll know how to try 100 percent to be their personal best. They wave good-bye to their teacher and set off on their journey.

Inch and Miles walk to the edge of the school yard. They stand for a bit wondering what will happen next. "I think you have to blow the whistle," Miles says. So Inch gives the whistle a loud HOOTIE-TOOT-TOOT!

Suddenly their school and all the noise of the school yard have disappeared. They hear footsteps, not louder nor larger than a grain of sand.

"Hey, you two! Watch out up there!" a voice shouts from far below.

Inch and Miles look down at the ground—way down. They spot a speck.

"Hey," the speck yells, "be careful! You almost squashed me flat."

The speck is a little ant.

Miles speaks first. "Excuse us, Mr. Ant, we're looking for clues to the Pyramid of Success. Can you help?"

"First of all, my name is Axelrod, not Mr. Ant," the ant replies. "And second, if you're looking for a clue to the Pyramid, follow me."

With that, the little ant disappears down a tiny hole in the ground.

"Uh-oh," says Inch. "Now what do we do? We're too big to follow Axelrod."

"The whistle!" shouts Miles. "Mr. Wooden's silver whistle. Give it another toot."

And that's just what Inch does.

HOOTIE-TOOT-TOOT!

And zippity-zap, quick as a nap, Inch and Miles are in a tiny dark tunnel, nose-to-nose with Axelrod.

"I'm busy," says the little ant. "So pay attention. Here's the first clue to the Pyramid."

Axelrod begins.

I may be small. That's very true.
But I Succeed, and so can you.
I move a mountain, bit by bit.
It takes Hard Work—I never sit.
I Work and Work throughout the day.
My Work comes first before I play.
Success is yours, please understand,
When you and Work go hand in hand.

Inch looks at Miles and yells, "I've got it. Hard Work is the first block of the Pyramid!"

"That's right," Miles replies. "Even someone as small as Axelrod can move a mountain if he works hard."

Inch and Miles turn to thank Mr. Wooden's friend. But Axelrod is gone. He's too busy to hang around. He has lots of Hard Work to do!

Happy to have discovered the first building block of the Pyramid, Inch gives the silver whistle a loud HOOTIE-TOOT-TOOT!

HARD WORK

ENTHUSIASM

Instantly, Inch and Miles find themselves perched atop a towering tree. Peppy as a parade on the Fourth of July, Rhonda the Robin lands on the branch next to them. She has a big smile on her beak.

Inch and Miles cling tightly as Rhonda cheerfully chirps a well-chosen clue.

I sing my song with joyful heart.
In your SUCCEss, joy plays a part.
Enthusiasm in your smile,
Combined with work, you'll find worthwhile.
The energy and pep you show
Will rub off on those you know.
Don't make excuses, complain, or whine.
Enjoy your work and SUCCEss you'll find.

With that, Rhonda flutters, flaps, and flies away.

Together, Inch and Miles exclaim, "Enthusiasm! That's the next block of the Pyramid. Smile, don't frown. Have pep and energy." The travelers are so excited, they lose their grip on the little branch and go tumbling head over paws and end over end toward the ground far below.

Miles yells, "Blow the whistle, Inch. Quick! Blow it loud and with Enthusiasm!"

HOOTIE-TOOT-TOOT! blares the shining silver whistle, and suddenly from out of nowhere, a long, hairy arm plucks Inch and Miles out of the air.

The hairy arm belongs to Charlie the Chimp. Charlie is swinging from tree to tree on a long vine looking for bright yellow bananas. As Inch and Miles swing along in Charlie's arm, he offers them the next clue to the Pyramid.

My friends are like a family.
I share with them. They share with me.
Respect your friends in all you do,
And they'll give back respect to you.
You'll find Success if this you learn:
The gift of Friendship must be earned.
To make a friend, I do believe,
That you, yourself, a friend must be.

"Friendship!" shouts Inch. "Friendship has to be the next block of the Pyramid."

"That's right," says Miles. "Friendship is earned by being a good friend."

Charlie grins as he sets the travelers down. Inch and Miles wave as Charlie swings off in search of bright yellow bananas to share with his friends.

NELLIE + J.W.

FRIENDSHIP

LOYALTY

To their great surprise, Inch and Miles find themselves next to a furry, slobbering sheepdog. Looking up from the bone he's gnawing on, Shep invites the travelers to join him for lunch. "Care for a little gnaw?" he barks to Inch and Miles.

"No thanks," they politely reply. (Inch and Miles like ice cream, not bones covered with drool.) "But can you help us? We want to learn how to try 100 percent to do our best."

The big slobbering sheepdog stops his gnawing and barks out a clue.

I'll wag my tail when you're feeling bad.
I'll cheer you up if you're kinda sad.
I'm honest and fair, and my word is true.
When others run out, I'll be there for you.
Loyalty's a trait built upon trust.
Others must see you as truthful and just.
I'm telling you now, when the going gets tough,
Loyalty's important. No amount is too much.

As Shep scampers off in search of a new bone, Inch says, "Miles, Shep is talking about Loyalty. Right?"

Miles is all smiles. "That's it! We must stick together and be honest and true. Loyalty is the next block of the Pyramid."

The travelers are happy with their new discovery, but Inch is very eager for another clue. HOOTIE-TOOT-TOOT! goes the silver whistle and bippity-boom, off they zoom.

"What's that buzzing?" Miles asks.

"Don't move," Inch warns, "or you'll get stung." The travelers stand as still as stones on a beehive swarming with bumblebees.

Amidst the drone, Inch and Miles hear a friendly voice. A bee with a smiling face emerges from the swarm.

"Welcome to our hive. I'm Betty, and I know why you're here," she buzzes. Inch and Miles are all ears as Betty buzzes them a clue.

I'm one of millions in our hive.
It looks confused as we all strive.
We buzz around throughout the day.
Cooperation's our sweet way.
Work as one in all you do.
When you help others, they'll help you.
Seek to know what someone needs.
Then pitch right in and you'll Succeed.

As Betty flits away in search of fresh flowers, Inch and Miles exclaim, "Cooperation is the next block of the Pyramid! Bees make honey by working together. They Cooperate!"

As Miles scoops up a handful of sweet, golden honey, Inch puckers up and blows another HOOTIE-TOOT-TOOT! on the amazing silver whistle.

COOPERATION

SELF-CONTROL

Splaaaash!

Deep underwater in a clear blue lake, Inch and Miles are swimming side by side. A beautiful, rainbow-colored trout swims in and out between them, tickling the travelers with her fins. "Follow me," Tess seems to be saying, as she swims straight down, leading Inch and Miles to the next clue. There in the sand at the bottom of the lake, they read:

If Success is your great goal,
You must practice Self-Control.
Use common sense in all you do.
Controlling emotions is helpful too.
I knew a fish who took the bait.
Good judgment gone, the hook he ate.
My friend was fried upon the grill,
With Self-Control, he'd be here still.

A knowing glance passes between Inch and Miles. Self-Control—that's another block! With each new clue they discover, they are getting closer to building the Pyramid of Success.

Uh-oh, thinks Inch. *We're running out of air.* And with that, Inch blows a soggy **GLUBTOOT, GLUBTOOT, GLUBTOOT!** and the two friends are on their way again.

Inch and Miles are standing in tall grass, dripping from their dip in the lake.

"Stop it!" Inch tells Miles. "That tickles."

"Stop what?" Miles asks, looking puzzled. "I'm not doing anything."

"Then who's tickling…" Inch begins, until he notices something twitching right in front of him. It's a nose doing the twitching and tickling. Rascal the Rabbit is attached to the nose.

"I'm just making sure that you're friendly," says the rabbit attached to the nose. "I can't be too careful, you know. There's a hungry fox in the neighborhood."

"Don't worry," Inch assures the rabbit with the twitching nose. "We're only looking for clues to the Pyramid of Success."

Rascal smiles and nods his big ears. "If it's clues you want, you've come to the right place. Now, pay attention." Then Rascal begins.

My ears are as tall as telephone poles.
My nose is like a button with holes.
I listen and look and sniff around.
I stay Alert to sights and sounds.
And one more thing that I should mention,
Alertness means you pay attention
To all the things that others share.
You'll learn so much if you're aware.

Inch and Miles like Rascal's clue. "Alertness is the next block," says Inch. "We must keep our eyes and ears open and pay attention."

"Don't forget our noses," adds Miles. "Smelling can help us learn too."

ALERTNESS

Inch adds, "In every way we must be Alert and keep learning. That really helps us be our best!"

Rascal's twitching nose suspects a hungry fox nearby. He dashes into the bushes as the silver whistle shrills another HOOTIE-TOOT-**TOOT!**

ACTION

Inch and Miles suddenly hear a very unusual noise. It's coming from a hole in a nearby walnut tree. Crunch, crunch, crunch. It's Skittles the Squirrel munching on a crunchy lunch. "Ummm, I love a nice fresh walnut. Deeeeelicious!" exclaims Skittles.

"Hey," shouts Inch above the crunch. "Can you take a break from cracking walnuts and help us with a clue to the Pyramid of Success?"

Skittles scurries down the tree. He's clearly hungry and in a hurry but agrees to share a clue. Inch and Miles pay close attention as Skittles wipes a few walnut crumbs off his chin and begins.

I scurry 'round and 'round each day.
Taking Action is my way.
I get up and go and give it my all.
When Action's needed, I never stall.
And when I look for lunch to eat,
I'm not afraid to risk defeat.
Don't fear failure. Try your best.
Take some Action for Success.

Miles pipes up, "Hey, that's right. Action means you can't just sit around and watch TV all day. You have to get up and do something!"

Skittles doesn't have time for idle chatter and ducks back into the hole to crack walnuts.

Inch doesn't waste time either. He takes Action. HOOTIE-TOOT-TOOT! And off the travelers go.

"Whoa," cries Miles. "This lily pad is as slippery as soap. Hang on, Inch."

"Ribbit," croaks a small green frog on a nearby lily pad. "I'm Fred."

Inch isn't sure how much longer he can stay on the lily pad without sliding off, so he gets right to the point. "Fred, we're looking for a clue to Mr. Wooden's Pyramid of Success. Can you help us?"

Fred stays very still—he doesn't want to scare away any bugs—and croaks out a clue.

Patiently I wait and wait,
Knowing that a bug tastes great.
Wait I will 'til a bug is mine,
Because Success, of course, takes time.
It's Determination I must show
To get the bugs I need to grow.
So when a bug comes whizzing by,
I snap my tongue and good-bye fly.

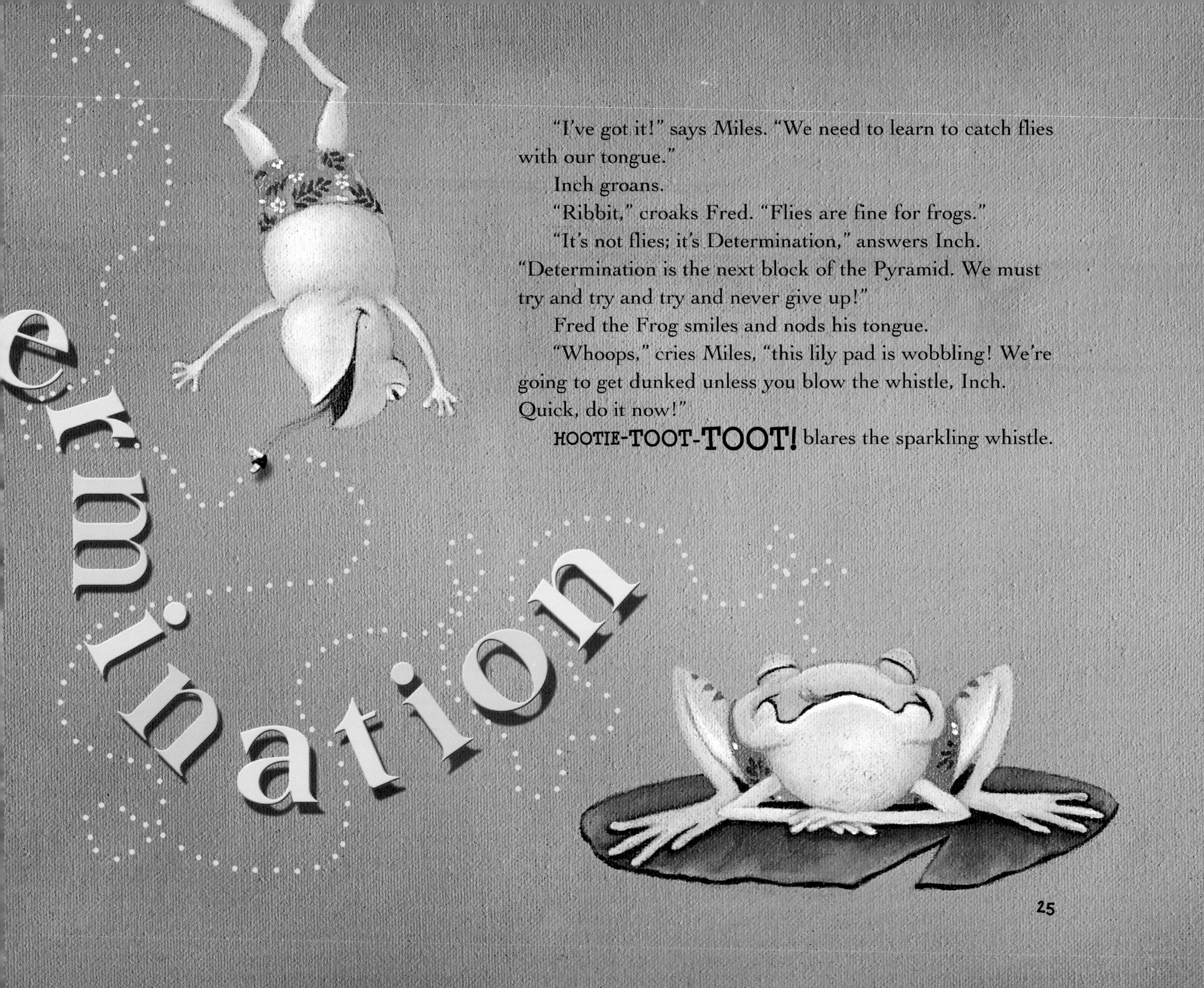

"I've got it!" says Miles. "We need to learn to catch flies with our tongue."

Inch groans.

"Ribbit," croaks Fred. "Flies are fine for frogs."

"It's not flies; it's Determination," answers Inch. "Determination is the next block of the Pyramid. We must try and try and try and never give up!"

Fred the Frog smiles and nods his tongue.

"Whoops," cries Miles, "this lily pad is wobbling! We're going to get dunked unless you blow the whistle, Inch. Quick, do it now!"

HOOTIE-TOOT-**TOOT!** blares the sparkling whistle.

Clippity-clop, clippity-clop, clippity-clop.

Inch and Miles are bouncing up and down on the back of a sleek racehorse.

"Whoa," Miles cries. "We don't know how to drive a horse." The horse slows down to a clip-clop, clip-clop, clip-clop.

Inch leans over to whisper in the horse's big ear. "We are looking for Success. Can you help us?"

"Listen closely," Hugh the Horse whinnies.

To run a race and do my best,
I exercise to pass the test.
I get my sleep and eat good food.
Healthy thoughts improve my mood.
When I am fit to run the race,
The other horses I can outpace.
Your Fitness level must be great.
Success requires a healthy state.

"Fitness!" shouts Miles.

Inch smiles and adds, "We must eat good food, think good thoughts, and get plenty of rest. That's a big part of being our personal best. Fitness is the next block of the Pyramid."

Hugh's race is about to begin. Without warning, the fit racehorse bucks Inch and Miles into the air. Flipping head over paws, Miles shouts, "Time to blow the silver whistle, Inch. Right now!"

HOOTIE-TOOT-TOOT!

FITNESS

Inch and Miles are all tangled up.

"Inch, we're caught in a fishing net. Somebody must think we're flying fish!" cries Miles. "Now what are we going to do?"

A nearby voice says smoothly, "Don't worry. You're not caught in a fishing net. Welcome to my web. I'm Silky the Spider."

Inch and Miles stop trying to untangle themselves as Silky begins to spin out another clue.

To weave a web demands great Skill,
And snaring lunch is quite a thrill.
Practice makes my webs grow finer.
I'm a top-notch web designer.
I pay attention to each detail.
I do it right so I won't fail.
I learned my Skill through hours of drill.
To find Success, you must have Skill.

"I've got it!" shouts Inch. "Skill is Silky's building block."

Miles nods and adds, "Silky pays attention to details and practices hard. Skill is a big part of the Pyramid of Success."

"We're getting to the top of the Pyramid," says Miles. "But we won't get there if we're all tangled up like this."

Inch struggles with tangled arms to grab the whistle. HOOTIE-TOOT-TOOT! and off they scoot.

"Grrrrrrrrr!" growls a gravelly, gruff voice. "You're very brave to come here." Looming over Inch and Miles is a ferocious-looking lion.

"We don't want to be your lunch. We need your help," cries Miles.

"And we want to be your friend," adds Inch, just to be safe.

Together they explain. "We're searching for the final clues to Mr. Wooden's Pyramid of Success."

Louie the Lion growls a friendly growl. "Your teacher is my friend. When I was a cub, he taught me this important block from his Pyramid of Success."

The team comes first, I must confide.
I'm always eager to help the pride.
I'll sacrifice my own desires
And do for them what is required.
Your team is part of who you are.
But don't forget, the team's the star.
You help, support, and then you cheer it.
To find Success, show strong Team Spirit.

Inch and Miles look up at Louie. His teeth are long and his breath is bad, but his clue is good.

"Team Spirit is being eager to do what's best for the team. That's important if you want to try to do your best," says Miles.

Louie growls in agreement but adds, "You better run along. It's almost lunchtime, and I *am* getting hungry."

Miles is pretty sure that Louie is joking. Nevertheless, Inch quickly blows on the whistle. HOOTIE-TOOT-TOOT! And off they go!

GO TEAM
GO TEAM
TEAM SPIRIT

POISE

"What a view!" shouts Miles. "We can see forever from up here."

Inch and Miles are hanging from the talons of a high-flying eagle. Everett is soaring above the clouds with Inch and Miles along for the view.

"I hope you're not afraid of heights," Everett warns.

"No, but please don't let go," Miles shouts above the wind. "We can flap, but we can't fly."

Everett zooms above the earth like a feathery kite. Proudly, he offers the next clue to Mr. Wooden's Pyramid.

I'm Everett the Eagle flying free.
There's no one else who's quite like me.
And there's no one who's quite like you.
So be yourself 'cuz you are cool.
With Poise you like the one you are.
It gives you pride and takes you far.
Poise is needed for Success.
Just be yourself; "yourself" is best!

"Poise is a new word and I like it," Miles admits. "It just means to be yourself."

"That's right," agrees Inch. "We're each special. We're each good. We each should like who we are!"

A big smile spreads across Everett's beak. Then without warning, he opens his claws.

"Ohhhhhhhhhhhh," yells Miles as he and Inch drop like rocks through the air. "Blow the whistle! Blow the whistle!" he yells.

As the earth comes rushing up faster and faster, the silver whistle blasts a mighty **HOOTIE-TOOT-TOOT!**

The long scaly rock that Inch and Miles are standing on starts to move.

"Why does this rock have eyes?" asks Miles.

"Why does this rock have a nose?" questions Inch.

"I'm not a rock. I'm an alligator," a voice rumbles.

Inch and Miles are standing on the long, hard nose of Albert the Alligator.

"I think I'm gonna sneeze," says Albert. "You're tickling my nose."

"Wait!" the two friends exclaim. "Don't sneeze. We need the final clue to Mr. Wooden's Pyramid. Please tell us before you sneeze!"

Albert's eyes are watering. Albert's nose is tickling. Albert can feel a mighty big sneeze on the way. But first, Albert gives Inch and Miles the final clue to the Pyramid.

Many are taller. Others run faster.
To race with most would be a disaster.
But I don't care if they seem greater.
I trust in me, the alligator.
My Confidence is plain to see.
I have learned to trust in me.
The Pyramid will teach you too.
Be Confident; believe in you!

"Confidence!" exclaims Inch. "That's the final block of the Pyramid. Don't be afraid if others seem bigger or better or braver. Be Confident and believe in yourself!"

"Hooray!" they shout, jumping up and down on Albert's sensitive snout. And that's all it takes. Albert lets forth a gigantic alligator sneeze. **"Koo-Koo-Ka-Chooooooo–Kachoo!"** Inch and Miles fly off Albert's nose like rockets shot into space.

GATORS RULE
CONFIDENCE

For what seems like a long, long time, Inch and Miles sail through creamy cotton clouds. They hear strange sounds like thunder in a bottle, rain in a teakettle, and lightning crackling upside down and sideways.

So much is happening that Inch and Miles close their eyes and cover their ears. Where are they going? What will happen next?

KaTHUD! Inch and Miles land with a thump and a bump.

"Welcome back!"

The familiar voice tells Inch and Miles that they are back with their favorite teacher.

"It's Mr. Wooden," they shout with glee. And what they see in the classroom makes them even happier. It's his Pyramid of Success! All the blocks are in place. From Axelrod's Hard Work to Albert's Confidence and all the blocks in between.

As Inch gives the shining silver whistle to Mr. Wooden, the wise old teacher asks his two students a familiar question, knowing that this time they'll know the answer. "So, Inch and Miles, what is Success?" Mr. Wooden asks.

Together they reply:

Success isn't having trophies or toys.
It isn't a medal or friends of your choice.
What is Success? That's easy to see.
It's trying to be the best *you* can be!
Don't worry what others may have or might say.
When trying your best,
Success comes your way.

PERSONAL BEST

POISE
Just be yourself.

CONFIDENCE
You must believe in yourself if you expect others to believe in you.

FITNESS
Act, eat, and think right.

SKILL
Practice makes perfect.

TEAM SPIRIT
Be eager to help your team.

SELF-CONTROL
Control yourself so others won't have to.

ALERTNESS
What you learn after you know it all is what counts.

ACTION
Be quick, but don't hurry.

DETERMINATION
Slow and steady gets you ready.

HARD WORK
Failing to prepare is preparing to fail.

FRIENDSHIP
To make friends, be a friend.

LOYALTY
Be trustworthy.

COOPERATION
Be more interested in finding the best way, not in having your way.

ENTHUSIASM
Make each day special.

Inch and Miles are pleased. They have discovered the meaning of true Success. And summer vacation is about to begin! What could be better? As the final school bell rings, Inch and Miles head toward the classroom door. But before they leave, they turn and thank their teacher. "See you next year, Mr. Wooden. Have a great summer. And thank you for teaching us about the Pyramid of Success."

Then Inch and Miles race out to play with their friends.

Mr. Wooden smiles a great big smile. He is happy too. Teaching kids about Success is what he loves to do most of all. "It's simple," he says to the now empty classroom. "Just follow the Pyramid." He gives the shining silver whistle a soft hootie-toot-toot! Then he wraps it in the tattered green cloth and carefully places it back into the drawer of his old oak desk.

Inch and Miles may be ready for summer vacation, but their wise old teacher is ready for a nap. It's been a long and successful day.

ore interested in finding the best way, not in having your way ✳ Control yourself so others won't have to ✳ What you learn after you kn
steady gets you ready ✳ Act, eat, and think right ✳ Practice makes perfect ✳ Be eager to help your team ✳ Just be yourself ✳ You must

to prepare is preparing to fail ✳ Make each day special ✳ To make friends, be a friend ✳ Be trustworthy ✳ Be more interested in finding
ry ✳ Slow and steady gets you ready ✳ Act, eat, and think right ✳ Practice makes perfect ✳ Be eager to help your team ✳ Just be yours